Paddington

at the Palace

First published in hardback in Great Britain by HarperCollins*Publishers* in 1986
First published in paperback by HarperCollins Picture Lions in 2001
Revised paperback editions published by HarperCollins *Children's Books* in 2010, 2015 and 2019
This edition published in 2022

HarperCollins *Children's Books* is a division of HarperCollins*Publishers* Ltd
1 London Bridge Street, London SE1 9GF

www.harpercollins.co.uk

HarperCollins*Publishers*
1st Floor, Watermarque Building, Ringsend Road, Dublin 4, Ireland

10

ISBN: 978-0-00-832604-3

Printed in the UK

MIX
Paper from
responsible sources
FSC® C007454

FSC is a non-profit international organisation established to promote the responsible management of the world's forests. Products carrying the FSC label are independently certified to assure consumers that they come from forests that are managed to meet the social, economic and ecological needs of present and future generations.

Find out more about HarperCollins and the environment at
www.harpercollins.co.uk/green

Michael Bond
Paddington
at the Palace

Illustrated by R. W. Alley

HarperCollins *Children's Books*

One morning Paddington and Mr Gruber set out to see the Changing of the Guard at Buckingham Palace.

Mr Gruber took his camera, Paddington took a flag on a stick in case he saw the Queen, and they both sat on the front seat of the bus so that they could see all the places of interest on the way.

The bus took them most of the way, then they had to walk through St James's Park.

It was a lovely sunny morning and there were flowers everywhere.

"I think I may pick some for the Queen," said Paddington.

"I'm afraid that's against the law," said Mr Gruber. "This is what is known as a Royal Park, and all the flowers belong to the Queen anyway. Besides, it would spoil it for others.

"If you like I'll take a picture for your scrapbook instead."

"Fancy having a front garden as big as this," said Paddington. "I wonder if she has to mow the lawn?"

Mr Gruber laughed and then, as they drew near to some large gates, he pointed towards the roof of a building behind them.

"We're in luck's way, Mr Brown," he said. "There's a flag flying. That means the Queen is at home."

Paddington peered through the railings and waved his own flag
several times in case the Queen was watching.

"I think I saw someone at one of the windows, Mr Gruber,"
he called excitedly. "Do you think it was the Queen?"

"Who knows?" said Mr Gruber.

Soon afterwards they heard the sound of a band playing. The music got louder and louder and there was a lot of shouting and the *clump, clump* of marching feet.

But by then there were so many people,
Paddington couldn't see a thing.

Mr Gruber wondered
whether he ought
to suggest holding
Paddington up to see,
but in the end he bought
him a periscope instead.

"If you look through the
bottom end," he explained,
"you can see over the top of
people's heads."

Paddington tried it out, but
all he could see were other
people's faces and he didn't
think much of some of those.

In the end he tried crawling through the legs of the crowd,
but by the time he got to the other side the band had passed by.

"Look," said a small boy, pointing at Paddington. "One of the soldiers has dropped his hat."

"It's what they call a busby, dear," said his mother.

Paddington jumped to his feet. "I'm not a *busby*," he cried. "I'm a bear!"

Gradually the crowd melted away until there were only a few people left.

"Oh dear," said Mr Gruber. "It's all over and I didn't even get a picture of you with one of the guardsmen."

"I didn't even *see* them," said Paddington sadly.

Just then a man in a bowler hat said something to a policeman by the gate, and then pointed towards Paddington and Mr Gruber.

The policeman beckoned to them. "I've instructions to invite you inside so that you can take a proper photograph," he called. "You're very honoured."

Paddington felt most important as he and Mr Gruber followed the policeman across the Palace parade ground and the guard came to attention.

"I think," he said, as he stood to attention while Mr Gruber took
a photograph, "this guard is so good he doesn't need changing."

As they left the Palace, Paddington stopped by the gates to wave his flag.

"Do you think it was the Queen looking out of the window when we first came?" he asked.

"It was either the Queen," said Mr Gruber, "or it was someone who likes bears very much."

And he took one last picture for Paddington's scrapbook. "You must mark the window with a cross when you paste it in – just in case."

me at the Palace.

Collect more fantastic books about

Paddington

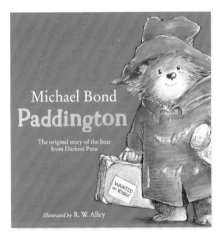

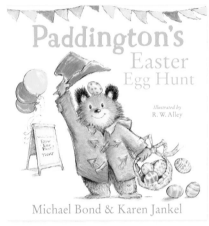

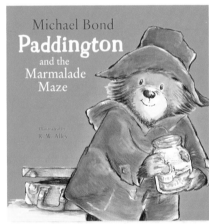

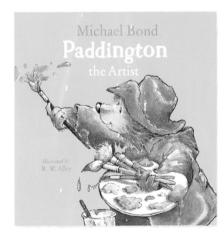

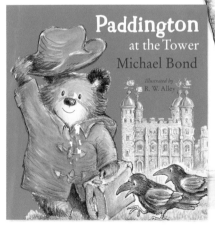

More than 35 million Paddington books sold worldwide!